Ella's Birthday Surprise

GROSSET & DUNLAP
Penguin Young Readers Group
An Imprint of Penguin Random House LLC

Based on "By Invitation Only" from the animated television series *Ella the Elephant*. Written by Scott Albert.
ELLA THE ELEPHANT™ and all related logos and characters are trademarks of DHX Cookie Jar Inc.
Ella the Elephant © 2013 CJ Ella Productions Inc. DHX MEDIA® DHX Media Ltd.

© 2015 DHX Cookie Jar Inc. Book adapted by Amy Ackelsberg. Published by Grosset & Dunlap, an imprint of Penguin Random House LLC,
345 Hudson Street, New York, New York 10014. GROSSET & DUNLAP is a trademark of Penguin Random House LLC. Printed in the USA.

ISBN 978-0-448-48925-4   10 9 8 7 6 5 4 3 2 1

It was the day before Ella's birthday, and she couldn't wait to celebrate.

"I'm so excited for my birthday," Ella said to her mom in the bakery. "It's all I can think about!"

"Why don't you go play in the park?" her mom suggested. "That might help take your mind off it."

Ella went to the park
and saw her friends there.
"Hi, guys! Want to play a
game?" she said.
"Um, uh . . . I have to go!"
Tiki replied.

"I think I hear my mom calling me!" said Frankie. "Bye!"

"We have to go, too. Bye, Ella!" said Ada and Ida.

Ella watched her friends hurry away. She wondered why they were acting so strange. They didn't even mention her birthday!

Ella saw her friend Belinda
on the other side of the park.
"Hi, Belinda!" Ella said.
"Oh, hi, Ella," Belinda answered,
looking a bit surprised. "Isn't it such a
nice day to, uh, stand in the park . . .
doing, uh, nothing suspicious?"

"Um, sure, Belinda," Ella replied, confused. "But not as nice as tomorrow will be!"

"Tomorrow?" said Belinda. "Oh, right. Tomorrow, my dad, the mayor, is getting a haircut!"

"Okay . . . ," said Ella. "Well, I have to go help my mom in the bakery. See you later, Belinda!"

On her way home, Ella wondered why no one seemed to remember her birthday. Then, she had an idea.

"I know!" she said. "I'll throw myself the best birthday party ever! All my friends can come, and they'll never forget my birthday again!"

Ella's friends had other plans. That afternoon, they met at Belinda's house to plan Ella's surprise party.

"Gather around for your party assignments," Belinda said. "And remember, *don't let Ella find out*!"

Meanwhile, Ella was shopping for her own birthday celebration.

She went to buy balloons and party supplies, but the store had nothing left.

Hmm, that's weird, Ella thought.

Ella walked to another store and saw Belinda and Tiki pulling a large wagon.

"Hi, Belinda! Hi, Tiki!" she said. "What are you doing?"

"Oh, hi, Ella! We're just getting supplies for my dad's, um, haircut party," Belinda replied. "Well, gotta run!"

"Hmm, that's strange," Ella said as her friends walked away.

11

Back at the bakery, Ella's mom and Belinda were discussing the cake for Ella's surprise birthday party.

"I just hope she'll be surprised," Ella's mother told Belinda.

Just then, Ella arrived at the bakery.

"Surprise?" asked Ella. "What surprise?"

"Ella!" her mom exclaimed. "I didn't know you were coming back so soon!"

"This cake is for, um . . . to celebrate my dad's haircut!" Belinda said.

"Do you always get a cake when your dad gets a haircut?" asked Ella.

"Um, well . . . It's a very special haircut! See you later, Ella!" Belinda answered, leaving the bakery.

"It sounds like Mayor Blue's haircut is going to be more fun than my birthday," Ella told her mom.

"What do you mean?" her mom asked.

"My friends seem to have forgotten my birthday, so I decided to throw myself a party. But everywhere I went, they were out of party supplies!" Ella explained.

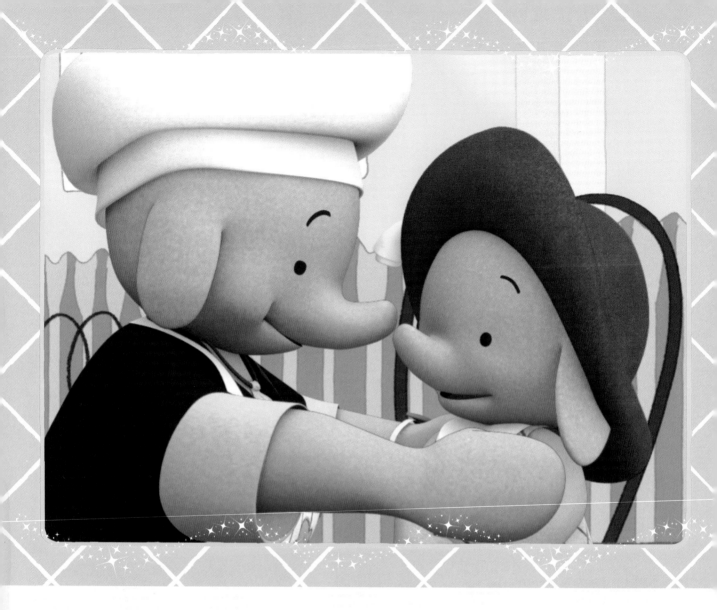

"Oh, Ella, tomorrow you and I will do something really special for your birthday,"
Ella's mom said and gave her a hug.

"Thanks, Mom," Ella replied, cheering up a little. "I know my birthday will be fun,
no matter what!"

The next morning, Ella woke up bright and early.

"Yay! It's my birthday!" Ella exclaimed. "I just wish my friends hadn't forgotten."

"Happy birthday, Ella!" her mom said, giving her a hug. "Are you sure your friends forgot?"

"Hmm . . . I guess *don't* know for sure," she replied. "I'll go to Belinda's and find out!"

Oh dear, her mother said to herself as Ella ran down the street. *I hope Ella's friends are ready with that surprise party!*

Ella rang the bell at Belinda's house.

"Hello, Mayor Blue," said Ella. "Is Belinda here?"

"Hi, Ella! Belinda will be with you in a minute," the mayor answered. "Is everything okay? You look a little sad."

"I think my friends forgot my birthday today," said Ella.

"Well, I have something very important to show you," he replied. "Follow me!"

Ella and Mayor Blue walked toward the kitchen. But when the mayor tried to open the kitchen door, it was locked.

"Oh no! I don't have the key!" he exclaimed.

"Do we really need to get into the kitchen right now?" asked Ella.

"Yes, we do!" said the mayor.

"I've got an idea, then," Ella said. "Magic hat, here we go!" Ella tossed her hat into the air, and it turned into a key! Ella unlocked the door and . . .

"Surprise!" her friends and family exclaimed. "Happy birthday!"

"You didn't forget about my birthday, after all!" Ella said.

"Of course not! We wanted to give you a special surprise!" Belinda explained.

"And here's your birthday cake, Ella!" said her mom. "Make a wish!"

"All I wanted was to celebrate my birthday with my family and friends, so my wish already came true!" Ella said as she blew out her candle.

24